Miss Small Is Off the Wall!

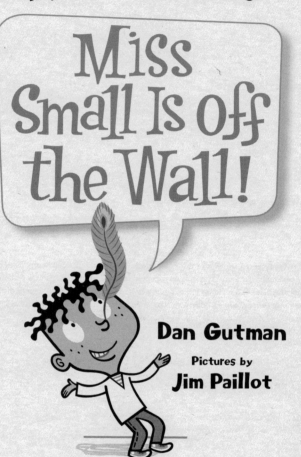

Miss Small Is off the Wall!

Dan Gutman

Pictures by Jim Paillot

HarperTrophy®
An Imprint of HarperCollinsPublishers

Library of Congress Cataloging-in-Publication Data is available.
ISBN 0-06-074518-5 (pbk.)—ISBN 0-06-074519-3 (lib. bdg.)

❖

First Harper Trophy edition, 2005

Visit us on the World Wide Web!
www.harperchildrens.com

18 19 20 BRR 50 49 48 47 46

To Emma

Contents

Fizz Ed Is
the Coolest

My name is A.J. and I hate school.

Well, I hate that reading and writing and arithmetic part of school, anyway. That stuff is for the birds!

There's only one thing about school that I like.

Fizz Ed.

Fizz Ed! I *love* Fizz Ed! Fizz Ed is the coolest! Fizz Ed isn't even like school at *all*. Fizz Ed is what you would be doing if you didn't have to *go* to school. If you ask me, school would be cool if we could just have Fizz Ed all day long and forget about all that boring reading and writing and arithmetic stuff.

Well, actually, to be honest, I've never had Fizz Ed. At my school, the Ella Mentry School, we didn't have Fizz Ed last year when we were in first grade. But my friend Billy around the corner goes to a different school. Billy's in third grade, and he told me that at his school they play dodgeball and basketball and football in Fizz Ed. They get to do anything they want.

Man, I wish I could go to Billy's school instead of boring old Ella Mentry School. I've been waiting forever until I got to second grade, when we would have Fizz Ed.

"Okay, everybody, it's time to line up," my teacher, Miss Daisy, announced one morning after we pledged the allegiance.

"Line up for what?" we all asked.

"Fizz Ed!" Miss Daisy said. "We're going to meet Miss Small in the gym."

"Yippee!"

Smarty-pants and Dumbhead

"Yippee!" I shouted.

"Hooray!" shouted my friends Ryan and Michael. We all whooped and hollered and high-fived each other. Finally we could go to Fizz Ed and leave all that reading and writing and arithmetic behind for a change. Miss Daisy gave each of us a

4

name tag so Miss Small, the Fizz Ed teacher, would know who we were.

"What's Fizz Ed?" asked this girl who has red hair named Emily (well, actually the *girl* is named Emily, not her hair). "Are we going to learn about soda pop?"

Me and Ryan and Michael slapped our own heads. We couldn't believe it. That

was like the stupidest thing anybody ever said in the history of the world.

"Fizz Ed is gym class, dumbhead!" I told Emily. "Everybody knows that."

Emily looked all upset like she was going to start crying. That girl cries at any old thing.

"A.J.!" Miss Daisy said with her mean face. "Hold your tongue!"

"Okay."

So I stuck out my tongue and held onto it. Everybody laughed. Well, everybody but Emily and Miss Daisy.

The whole class lined up in size order so Miss Daisy could walk us over to the gym, which is all the way at the other end of the school. Ryan was the line leader.

"I bet Miss Small will let us play football and baseball and hockey and dodgeball," Michael whispered to me as we walked. Michael and Ryan are really good at sports. They're the best athletes in the second grade.

"Sports are cool," I said.

"Except for curling," said Michael. "That's just dumb."

"That's not even a sport," I said. "Curling is what girls do to their hair."

This girl with curly brown hair named

Andrea Young must have heard me, because she laughed even though I didn't say anything funny.

"Curling is *too* a sport," she said. "I saw it in a book about the Olympics. They take this big rock and slide it down the ice while somebody sweeps the ice in front of it with a broom."

Andrea thinks she is so smart. She probably goes home after school and reads the dictionary for fun. That way she can brag about how much she knows.

"You don't know anything about sports," I told Andrea.

"Do too," Andrea said back at me. "I

take a dance class every day after school. I'm learning ballet, jazz, tap, hip-hop, and clog dancing."

Andrea is one of those kids who takes lessons in everything. All she has to do is sneeze and her mother probably signs her up for sneezing lessons.

"Dancing is not a sport," I said. "Dancing is dumb."

"A little less chitchatting in the hall, please," said Miss Daisy as we walked to the gym.

"Do we really have to go to Fizz Ed, Miss Daisy?" asked Andrea. "Isn't it more important for us to learn reading, writing, and arithmetic?"

"Strong mind, strong body," said Miss Daisy.

Ha-ha-ha! Smarty-pants Andrea Young was gonna to have to do something *she* didn't like for a change. She wouldn't be the best in the class for a change. Welcome to my world, Andrea!

I couldn't wait to beat Andrea at basketball. Beat her at baseball. Beat her at football. This was going to be the greatest day in my life!

Andrea Young probably doesn't even know the difference between a football and a footprint.

Finally, after walking about a hundred miles, we reached the gym. It's this giant room with a basketball hoop at each end.

"Miss Small?" called Miss Daisy. "Are you here?"

Nobody answered, but there was an echo in the gym so we could hear Miss Daisy's words over and over again when they bounced off the walls.

"Miss Small? . . . Miss Small? . . . Miss Small? . . . Miss Small? . . . Are you here? . . . Are you here? . . . Are you here?"

It was cool.

"Hello!" I yelled.

The gym yelled back, "Hello! . . . Hello! . . . Hello! . . . Hello! . . . Hello!"

"Echo!" yelled Michael.

"Echo . . . echo . . . echo . . . echo," yelled the gym.

"A.J. is stupid!" yelled Ryan.

"A.J. is stupid! . . . A.J. is stupid! . . . A.J. is stupid! . . . A.J. is stupid!" yelled the gym.

I was gonna yell, "Ryan is a dumb-head," but instead Miss Daisy yelled, "Stop that, boys!"

"Stop that, boys! . . . Stop that, boys! . . . Stop that, boys!" yelled the gym.

It was cool.

At that very moment, somebody came running out of the office at the other end of the gym. It was the most amazing thing any of us had ever seen.

It was Miss Small.

Fun, Fun, Fun with Miss Small

Miss Small was carrying a basketball, a football, a soccer ball, a kickball, and just about every other kind of ball you could name. She ran out and climbed up on the bleachers. Then she jumped off the bleachers and jumped on one of those little trampolines on the floor.

14

She did a flip, went flying through the air, and tried to dunk all those balls in the basketball hoop. One or two of them went in, but mostly they went flying all over the place.

So did Miss Small. She landed in a heap on the floor.

Miss Small is off the wall!

"Are you okay?" we all asked as we gathered around her. I was afraid she might have broken something, because she was just lying there without moving.

"I'm fit as a fiddle!" Miss Small replied. "I just wanted to show you how you're *not* supposed to behave in the gym. In Fizz Ed, safety is our biggest concern."

Miss Daisy said she had to go back to class, and she left. Miss Small stood up slowly. It was amazing! Nobody could do anything except stare at her with their mouth open.

"Wow!" we all said.

The amazing thing was that Miss Small

was really *tall*! Like, she was a million inches big. Her head just about reached the basketball hoop. It was like a giant had walked into the room. She must be the tallest person in the history of the world!

Miss Small was the opposite of her name. It was like a fat guy was named Mr. Thin or a dumb guy was named Mr. Smart or a really handsome guy was

named Mr. Ugly or . . . well, you get the idea.

Miss Small blew into the shiny silver whistle that was hanging around her neck.

"Hey, kids! Are you ready to have some fun?"

"Yeah!" we all hollered.

"We're going to have lots of fun in Fizz Ed!" she said. "Fun fun fun, all the time! That's my motto."

"What's a motto?" asked Ryan.

"I don't know," Miss Small said. "What's a motto with you?"

Then she laughed.

"Do you like to play games?" Miss Small asked. "I *love* playing games!"

"I like to play video games," one of the boys said.

"Those aren't the kind of games I'm talking about," said Miss Small. "*Real* games are even more fun. I'm talking about running and jumping and chasing games. We're going to play Red Light Green Light, Red Rover, Spud, Mother May I, Duck Duck Goose. . . ."

"Those games are lame," Ryan whispered in my ear.

"Kids can get hurt when they run and jump and chase each other," said Andrea. "My mother told me to always be careful so I don't get hurt."

"Can you possibly be any more

boring?" I asked Andrea.

She is gonna make a great grown-up when she grows up. She's only eight, and she's already mature, which is a fancy way to say boring.

"Do we have to play games where somebody loses?" asked that crybaby Emily. "I think the team that loses should win too. My dad told me I'm a winner whether I win or lose."

"Your dad is weird," I said, even though Emily looked like she might cry again. "If everybody wins, what's the point of playing the game? That's why you play. To beat the other team."

"Competing is icky," said Andrea.

"It doesn't matter if you win or lose, A.J. It's how you play the game that counts," said Miss Small. "In Fizz Ed, our goal is to have fun and build strong, healthy bodies. But most of all, by the end of the term, I want you all to have cooties."

"Cooties!" everybody shrieked.

"Girls have cooties!" shouted all the boys.

"Boys have cooties!" shouted all the girls.

I never really knew what cooties were, but I knew they were something horrible that you wouldn't want to get.

"*Everybody* should have cooties," said Miss Small. "Cooties stands for COOperation, TEAmwork, and Sportsmanship."

Oh. I didn't care much about that stuff. I just wanted to beat Andrea Young at something because she thinks she is so smart. Besides, words that are made from the letters of other words are dumb.

Miss Small blew her whistle again.

"Before we do anything, we have to stretch."

Miss Small got down on the floor again and did some push-ups. Then *we* had to do push-ups. She did some sit-ups. Then *we* had to do sit-ups. She did some windmills and arm circles. Then *we* had to do windmills and arm circles.

"See if you can touch your toes," Miss Small said. "Now see if you can touch the sky. You want to be loose as a goose in a caboose."

Stretching was boring, and dumb, too. Nobody can touch the sky. After we stretched, Miss Small made us do about a million hundred jumping jacks.

"Isn't this fun?" Miss Small asked when we were finished.

I thought I was gonna throw up.

She blew her whistle again.

"Okay, now that we're all as loose as a goose in a caboose, who wants to play a game?"

"I do!" we all shouted.

Finally!

A Dumb Balancing Act

"Are we gonna play football?" I asked Miss Small.

"No," Miss Small said.

"How about basketball?" asked Ryan.

"Nope."

"Soccer?"

"Not even close."

"Baseball? Hockey? Tennis?"

"No. No. No."

"Curling?" I asked.

"No."

"I thought you said we were gonna have fun," Michael complained.

"I did," said Miss Small.

"So what are we gonna do?" I asked.

Miss Small went to a box near the bleachers and pulled out some giant feathers that were as long as her arms.

"We're going to balance these peacock feathers," she said.

"What!" I asked.

"Whoever can balance a feather on their finger the longest is the winner,"

Miss Small said. She took a feather and balanced it on her finger. "See, it's easy!"

She gave each of us a feather. I put the feather on my finger. It fell off right away. I put it back on my finger, and it fell off again. I tried moving my finger back and forth like Miss Small did to hold the feather up, but it fell off anyway.

Balancing feathers was not fun. It was dumb.

I looked up to see if Ryan could balance his feather. But his fell off. I turned around to see how Michael was doing. His feather fell off too.

In fact, there was only one kid in the whole class who was still balancing the dumb feather.

It was Andrea Young! Her dumb feather was just standing up all straight on her dumb finger like it was glued there.

"Good job, Andrea!" said Miss Small. "You have excellent balance." And she gave Andrea a certificate that said she was a feather-balancing expert.

"Thanks, Miss Small," Andrea said. "Maybe Fizz Ed won't be so bad after all!"

I hate her.

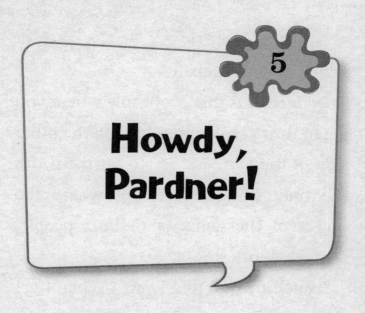

Howdy, Pardner!

After we were finished with that dumb stuff, Miss Small collected all the feathers and blew her whistle.

"Okay, let's have all the boys line up on one side of the gym and all the girls line up on the other side."

"All right!" I whispered to Ryan. "We're

gonna play dodgeball."

Dodgeball is this cool game where you get to throw balls at the kids on the other side of the gym and try to hit them. It's the only game I know of where the object of the game is to hurt people. Dodgeball rules!

"Watch this," I told Ryan. "When I get the ball, I'm gonna wham Andrea Young right in the head."

Me and Ryan high-fived. Then we switched places so I could be right across from Andrea. That way I could get a good shot at her.

The only problem was that Miss Small didn't go get any dodgeballs. When all the boys and girls were lined up on opposite sides of the gym, she went over to a boom box on the floor and turned it on. This annoying hillbilly music blasted out of the boom box. Miss Small put a big straw hat on her head and started dancing around like a lunatic.

"Yee-haw!" she hollered. "I reckon it's time for some square dancing!"

"What!" I shouted. "We're not supposed to dance in Fizz Ed. We're supposed to play ball and stuff. Square dancing is dumb."

But nobody could hear me because the girls were all whooping and squealing like they were opening their birthday presents or something.

"Everybody sashay to the middle of the gym and honor your partner!" Miss Small shouted. She was clapping her hands to the music.

I looked for Ryan and Michael, but they had already sashayed to the middle of the gym with the rest of the boys. I didn't want to be the only one standing there on the line, so I sashayed to the middle too.

"Howdy, pardner!" Andrea Young said to me, and she did one of those courtesy things girls do with their skirts.

No way I was gonna bow and say, "Howdy, pardner." I didn't want to honor

Andrea. I wanted to nail her in the head with a dodgeball.

"Swing your partner round and round!" shouted Miss Small.

Andrea grabbed my elbow and swung herself around me about a hundred million times.

"Hey, look!" Ryan shouted. "A.J. and Andrea are in *love*!"

"Shut up, Ryan!"

Then we all went back to our boy and girl places. I thought I was gonna throw up from all that spinning.

"Clap your hands!" ordered Miss Small.

"Circle left!" ordered Miss Small.

"Circle right!" ordered Miss Small.

"Now do-si-do!" ordered Miss Small.

"Do-si-what?" we all asked.

Miss Small showed us how to do-si-do, which is sort of like walking around somebody like you're pretending you don't see them. It was dumb.

I couldn't believe it. Instead of playing dodgeball or something cool with my friends, I had to do-si-do with Andrea Young. It wasn't fair.

"Isn't Fizz Ed fun, A.J.?" Andrea asked the next time we had to meet in the middle.

Why can't an asteroid fall on her?

After the square-dance disaster, Miss Small had us do the Chicken Dance. Now I don't know if they do the Chicken

Dance where you live, but it's the dumbest dance in the history of the world.

Everybody has to stand in a big circle and tuck their thumbs into their armpits. Then you have to flap your elbows like a chicken and cluck. Then you have to wiggle down to the floor and sing, "I don't want to be a chicken. I don't want to be a duck. So I shake my butt."

Really! Those are the words! If that's not dumb, I don't know what is. It was horrible.

When we finished the Chicken Dance, Miss Small showed us how to do somersaults. Then she ran all the way around the gym, and we had to follow her. I thought I was gonna die. Luckily she blew her whistle and told us that Fizz Ed was over for the day.

I couldn't wait to get out of there.

The Truth About Miss Small

At our school the cafeteria and the auditorium are the same room, so it's called the cafetorium. But all the kids call it the vomitorium ever since some kindergarten kid barfed in there last year.

I sit at a lunch table with Ryan and Michael and a few other boys. Andrea and Emily and some of their friends sit at the table next to ours. Sometimes for fun we peel the paper off our straws and shoot them at the girls. They usually laugh, except for the time I hit Emily in the face and she cried.

I gave my tuna sandwich to Ryan, and he gave me his Scooter Pie. Ryan will eat anything, even disgusting vegetables. One time me and Michael mixed up some milk and ketchup and mayonnaise in a cup. It was really gross, and I thought I was gonna throw up just looking at it. Ryan said he would drink it if we gave him a pack of baseball cards. So we gave him a pack of baseball cards and he drank it (the drink, not the baseball cards). Ryan is weird.

"That Miss Small must be seven feet tall," Ryan said.

"If I was as tall as she is," Michael said, "I wouldn't be a gym teacher. I'd be a professional basketball player."

"I would be a weatherman," Ryan said.

"Why?" I asked.

"Because when you're that tall, you can tell it's raining before anybody else. So you can predict the weather."

"Tall people can reach stuff on the top shelf without even having to stand on a chair, too," Michael said. "But I guess it must be really hard to tie your shoes

when you're so tall."

"She should tie her shoes first and *then* put them on," Ryan said.

At the table next to ours, Andrea Young turned around with her big dumb face.

"You can't tie your shoes and then put them on," she said.

"Can *too*," I said, and I shot my straw wrapper at Andrea. "I only tie my shoes once—the day my mom buys them. What's the point of untieing a shoe if you're just gonna have to tie it all over again the next day?"

"Yeah," Ryan and Michael agreed. Girls just don't have common sense.

"Boys are dumbheads," Andrea said,

giggling, and then she turned back to her own table. I wish a basketball backboard would crush her.

"I thought we were gonna be playing sports in Fizz Ed," Ryan complained. "When I saw how tall Miss Small was, I was sure she was gonna let us play basketball."

"Maybe she's not our Fizz Ed teacher at all," Michael said. "Did you ever think of that? Maybe she's a mutant alien freak from another planet where everybody is tall."

"Yeah," Ryan said. "Maybe she's a fake. Maybe she came to earth to kidnap our real Fizz Ed teacher and bring her back to her planet."

All of a sudden Emily turned around. Her face was all white.

"We've got to *do* something!" Emily said, and she ran out of the vomitorium.

Emily is weird.

Fizz Ed
Is Dumb

"Okay, everybody, it's time to line up,"
Miss Daisy announced later in the week.

"Line up for what?" we all asked.

"Fizz Ed!" Miss Daisy said.

"Yippee!" shouted all the girls.

"Boo!" shouted all the boys.

"What's the matter?" Miss Daisy asked.

"I thought you boys would love Fizz Ed."

"Fizz Ed is dumb," I told her. "All we do is balance feathers and square-dance."

Miss Daisy said we had to go to Fizz Ed anyway, and we walked a million hundred miles to the gym. Emily was the line leader, and I was the door holder.

"Good morning, boys and girls," said Miss Small. "Today we are going to do something really exciting. We're going to learn how to juggle scarves!"

"*What!*" I said. "You've gotta be kidding!"

But she wasn't. Miss Small grabbed a bunch of colorful scarves and gave three of them to each of us. Then she put on a little demonstration.

First she threw one scarf up in the air. Then she threw another one up in the air. Then she threw the third one up in the air. Then she caught the first one as it was falling and threw it back up in the air again. And she kept doing that with all three scarves over and over.

It looked pretty cool, I had to admit.

"How can you juggle three scarves with just two hands?" I asked.

"It's easy because the scarves float in the air," Miss Small said. "This will improve your eye-hand coordination. With a little practice, you'll be able to juggle three balls, or three clubs, or three of just about anything."

Miss Small blew her whistle and told us to give it a try. I threw a scarf up in the air, and then I threw another one. By the time I threw the third scarf up in the air, the first scarf had already fallen on the floor and the second scarf had landed on my head.

"My scarves are busted," I complained. "They don't float long enough. I need another set of scarves."

Miss Small gave me three more scarves, but the same thing happened. Every time I tried to grab a scarf out of the air, the other two were on the ground already.

Juggling scarves was dumb, I decided.

It wasn't a sport. They don't have any World Series for scarf juggling. There's no scarf-juggling Super Bowl. They don't give out any medals for scarf juggling in the Olympics. Juggling scarves was just about as dumb as curling.

I looked around to see how Ryan and Michael were doing. They weren't very good at juggling the dumb scarves either. In fact, there was only one kid in the whole class who was keeping all three scarves up in the air.

Andrea Young!

"Way to go, Andrea!" yelled Miss Small. "You have excellent eye-hand coordina-tion." Then she gave Andrea some certificate that said she was an expert scarf juggler.

"Thanks, Miss Small," Andrea said. "Juggling scarves is fun!"

I'll show *her* some eye-hand coordination. I'd like to coordinate my fist right into her eye.

Ghost in the Graveyard

When I got to school the next week, Ryan and Michael got to me as I was putting my backpack in my cubby.

"Check out you-know-who," they said.

At the front of the classroom, Andrea was juggling again. But she wasn't juggling scarves this time. She was juggling three *apples*! She had all of them up in the air at the same time. If it had been anybody else, I would have thought it was cool.

Andrea caught the apples and put them on Miss Daisy's desk as a present.

What a little brownnoser!

"Thank you, Andrea!" Miss Daisy said. "That was wonderful. How did you learn to juggle?"

"I practiced at home like Miss Small told us to," Andrea said. "It's easy!"

I hate her. She should go off and become a juggling clown in the circus.

"Okay, everybody, it's time to line up," Miss Daisy announced.

"Line up for what?"

"Fizz Ed!" Miss Daisy said.

"Yippee!" shouted all the girls.

"Boo!" shouted all the boys.

"I don't feel very good, Miss Daisy," I said.

"What's the matter, A.J.?" she asked.

"Do you have a tummy ache? A headache?"

I really felt fine. I just didn't want to go to Fizz Ed. But I didn't want to say that to Miss Daisy. I didn't know what to do. I didn't know what to say. I had to think fast.

"I think my tummy has a headache," I said, "or maybe it's my head that has a tummy ache." Everybody laughed, even though I didn't say anything funny.

"I know a cure for that," said Miss Daisy.

"Really?" I said.

"Sure. You'll feel fine after an hour of Fizz Ed."

We walked the million hundred miles to the gym. It was a really hot day, and I was already tired when we got there.

"Is everybody ready to play a game?" Miss Small asked. She was jumping up and down with excitement, like some little kid who never played a game before in her life.

"What do you think she's gonna have us do now," Ryan whispered to me, "spin plates on sticks?"

"I've got an idea for a game," I said, remembering to raise my hand.

"What game do

you want to play, A.J.?"

"How about chess?"

"Chess?" asked Miss Small. "Don't you want to play a game where you get to run around and jump up and down and have fun?"

"I'm a little tired of fun," I said.

"Yeah, having fun is too much work," Ryan said.

"How about we have a contest to see who can sit around and do nothing the longest?" suggested Michael.

"Oh, no. We're going to have lots of fun today," said Miss Small. "We're going to play a game called Ghost in the Graveyard."

"That sounds scary," said that crybaby Emily.

"It's not scary at all," Miss Small said. "It's fun! Let's go out to the playground."

So we all went out to the playground. Miss Small told us that the swings would be home base and that she would be the ghost.

"I'm going to hide," she said, "and you have to find me. The person who spots me yells 'Ghost in the graveyard!' and everybody has to run back to home base before I tag you. If I tag you before you get back to the swings, you become a ghost in the next round."

We all covered our eyes, and Miss

Small ran off to hide.

"One o'clock rock," we chanted. "Two o'clock rock . . . three o'clock rock . . . four o'clock rock . . ."

When we reached twelve o'clock, we all shouted "Midnight!" and uncovered our eyes.

"Where is she?" asked Michael. "I don't see her anywhere."

"She's hiding, silly!" Andrea said.

We looked all over for Miss Small. We looked by the monkey bars. We looked under the seesaw. We looked around the soccer goals. We looked by the basketball hoops. Miss Small had vanished.

It was hot out. We were tired from all

that looking. We sat in the shade of a tree to talk things over.

"Let me think," Andrea said. "If I was Miss Small, where would I be?"

"I played hide-and-seek with my dad once," Emily said. "I was looking for him for about an hour. And you know where I finally found him?"

"Where?" we asked.

"He was sitting on the couch in the living room watching a football game on TV."

"Cool," I said. "Who was playing?"

"Emily's point is that hiding games are just a way for grown-ups to *pretend* to play with us," Andrea explained. "They don't

really want to play. All they really want to do is sit around and do grown-up things."

"Grown-ups are so boring," I said.

"Miss Small is probably in the teachers' lounge," Ryan said. "I bet she's having a cup of coffee and talking about the weather or some other boring grown-up thing."

"Yeah!"

We were about to run to the teachers' lounge when I heard a cracking noise. It was almost like a creaking door in one of those scary movies.

"What's that?" I asked.

"What's what?" Michael asked.

The sound was coming from above. We all looked up. It was a big branch.

Not just a big branch. It was a big branch
with a person on it. And the person was
Miss Small!

"Watch out!" one of the girls screamed.

The branch with Miss Small on it was coming down right on top of us! She was screaming. So were we! We all dove out of the way.

"Ooof!" Miss Small grunted when she hit the ground.

"Ghost in the graveyard!" somebody shouted. And we all ran back to home base.

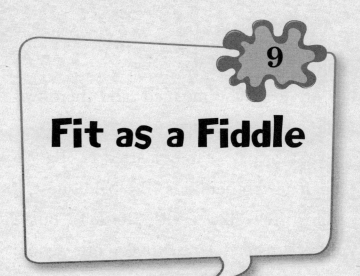

Fit as a Fiddle

9

Luckily for us, nobody got tagged by Miss Small on the way back to home base. Luckily for us, that is, but not so lucky for Miss Small. She was still lying there on the ground under the tree. So we all ran back to her.

"Are you okay?" we all asked as we

gathered around her.

"My leg," she moaned, and there was pain all over her face.

That crybaby Emily started crying. So did a few other kids. To be honest, I almost felt like crying myself. But I didn't. Instead I ran to get our school nurse, Mrs. Cooney.

Mrs. Cooney came running out of the school with a first-aid kit.

"Oh, dear!" Mrs. Cooney said when she saw Miss Small lying under the tree. She got down on her hands and knees to examine Miss Small.

"You should put a Band-Aid on her leg and kiss it," Michael told Mrs. Cooney.

"That's what my mom does when I get hurt."

"Your mom is weird," I told Michael.

"She's going to need more than a Band-Aid and a kiss," Mrs. Cooney told us. "This leg is broken."

Mrs. Cooney called for an ambulance on her cell phone, and it arrived just a couple of minutes later. Some guys got

out, and they put Miss Small on a stretcher and carried it into the ambulance. We asked them to put their siren on when they drove to the hospital, but they wouldn't. It was still cool anyway, having an ambulance right on the playground.

As soon as we got back to class, we all wrote get-well cards to Miss Small. They must have worked, because just a few days later, she was back at school. She had a big cast on her leg and crutches to help her walk. And she was smiling.

I thought Fizz Ed would be canceled for a few weeks until Miss Small got better. But the day after Miss Small was back, Miss Daisy told us to line up for Fizz Ed.

When we got to the gym, Miss Small was standing there with her crutches, waiting for us.

"I'm fit as a fiddle!" she said. "Let's have fun!"

Even though she was hobbling around, Miss Small still wanted to play games. We

played some more Ghost in the
Graveyard, but nobody was allowed to
climb the tree this time. Miss Small also

taught us how to play Red Light Green Light, Red Rover, Spud, London Bridge, Mother May I, and this really cool game called Duck Duck Goose.

I still wish we could have played basketball and football and baseball and sports like that. But those corny games Miss Small taught us were actually kind of fun, I had to admit.

Maybe Fizz Ed wasn't so bad after all.

10

Cooties and Clog Dancing

"Good morning, boys and girls," Principal Klutz said over the loudspeaker. "Today is Tuesday, and today is special because our own Miss Small is a quarter of a century old! So if you see Miss Small in the hall, be sure to wish her a happy birthday."

"Wow!" Ryan whispered to me. "A

quarter of a century is a long time."

After the morning announcements, we have this thing in our class called Show and Share. We have to bring in something from home and tell the class about it.

I brought in an old army helmet that my grandpa wore when he fought in a war a long time ago. It has fake leaves attached to it so Grandpa could hide in the woods and nobody would see him. I put it on my head even though it was too big for me. Then everybody passed the helmet around so they could feel how heavy it was.

"That's very interesting, A.J.," Miss Daisy said when I was finished. "It's your turn, Andrea. What do you have to share with us today?"

"That helmet is awesome, A.J.," Ryan whispered to me while Andrea got up.

"Yeah, let's see Andrea top *that*," I said.

Andrea lugged a big duffel bag up to the front of the class. She pulled three long sticks out of the bag. On the end of each stick was a thing that looked like a marshmallow, but black. Then she pulled out a lighter and set those marshmallow things on fire!

"My mom signed me up for juggling lessons," Andrea announced.

Then she threw those flaming sticks up in the air! I don't know how she did it,

but the sticks were flying all over the place. She kept catching them and throwing them back up in the air. If it had been anybody else, I would have thought it was super cool.

Finally Andrea caught all three sticks in one hand, blew them out, and took a bow. Everybody started cheering and clapping. I hate her.

"After I get good," Andrea said, "I'm going to learn how to juggle while I'm riding a unicycle."

I hope she rides her unicycle off a cliff.

"Okay, everybody, it's time to line up for Fizz Ed!" Miss Daisy announced.

When we got to the gym, we sang "Happy Birthday" to Miss Small and told her she didn't look half bad for somebody who had lived a quarter of a century.

"Today we're going to do something that's *really* fun!" Miss Small announced.

"Everybody choose a partner. We're going to have a three-legged race!"

"How can we have a three-legged race when we only have two legs?" I asked.

Everybody laughed even though I didn't say anything funny. I turned around to see if Ryan or Michael would be my partner. But Ryan chose Michael, and Michael chose Ryan.

Just about everybody had already chosen a partner. There was only one kid in the class besides me who didn't have a partner.

Andrea Young!

"Looks like we're partners, A.J.," Andrea said.

"Okay," I said. "But I'm not inviting you to my birthday party or anything."

"Don't worry, I'm not inviting you to my birthday party, either."

"Good."

Miss Small gave each team a piece of rope. We tied my left ankle to Andrea's right ankle. I had no place to put my left arm except around Andrea's shoulders. It was disgusting, but I had to do it.

"Hey, look!" Ryan said. "A.J. and Andrea are in *love*!"

Everybody laughed.

"Shut up, Ryan," I said.

"When are you gonna get married?" asked Michael.

Some friends! My face was all hot, and I would have beat up the two of them if I hadn't been tied to Andrea.

"A.J.," Andrea whispered, "I know how you can get back at Ryan and Michael."

"How?"

"Let's *beat* 'em!"

"Beat 'em?" I said. "Aren't you the one who said competing is icky?"

"I changed my mind," she said. "Let's beat 'em! Let's beat 'em bad! That will show 'em!"

"We can't beat 'em," I told her. "They're the best athletes in second grade. You're a girl."

"We can *do* it, A.J.!" Andrea said.

"Three-legged races are a lot like clog dancing."

"Clog dancing?" I asked. "Is that some dance that plumbers do when the sink gets clogged up?"

"No, silly. It's a step dance that you do with your heel keeping time with the music. I go clogging every Thursday after school."

"I'm not doing any clogging. Clogging is dumb."

"You want to win, don't you?" Andrea said. "Look, all you have to do is move your leg forward whenever I count to two."

"All right, all right," I said.

I didn't like the idea of Andrea Young ordering me around. But what else was I gonna do? Our legs were tied together.

Everybody lined up on the starting line.

"To win a three-legged race, you need cooties," Miss Small said. "Cooperation. Teamwork. Sportsmanship."

"Let's stomp 'em into the ground!" Andrea whispered in my ear. "Let's make 'em wish they were never born!"

"On your mark," Miss Small hollered. "Get set. Go!"

Me and Andrea took off.

"One . . . two . . . one . . . two . . ." Andrea said, "one . . . two . . . one . . . two . . ."

Andrea and I went clogging down the field. Some of the kids fell down. We were in first place. Ryan and Michael were right behind us.

"You'd make a great clogger, A.J.!" Andrea shouted.

"Quiet, I'm trying to concentrate!"

"One . . . two . . . one . . . two . . ."

Me and Andrea were out in front of everyone.

"One . . . two . . . one . . . two . . ."

Me and Andrea were pulling away from everybody else!

"One . . . two . . . one . . . two . . ."

Michael and Ryan fell down!

"One . . . two . . . one . . . two . . ."

Me and Andrea won the race!

"Ha-ha!" I called to Ryan and Michael. "Eat my dust, losers!"

I was so happy that I almost wanted to give Andrea a hug.

Almost.

Grown-ups Are Weird

Recess is the best time of the day because that's when we get to go out on the playground while the teachers do all the boring things grown-ups do when kids aren't around.

Lately Andrea was practicing her juggling during recess. She put on her dumb show, and kids in the other classes would gather around and watch. Like she was famous or something.

But today Andrea wasn't juggling. She and Emily were just sitting on the monkey bars looking all serious, like the world was about to end. Me and Michael and Ryan couldn't resist going over to bug them.

"What's the matter with you?" I asked Andrea. "Did you set your house on fire while you were juggling?"

"No," she said, "we're worried about Miss Small."

"What about her?" asked Ryan.

"We're afraid she might die," Emily said.

"What!" I said. "You're nuts! All she did was break her leg."

"Miss Small is a quarter of a century old," Andrea said. "That's like, ancient. Old ladies aren't supposed to run around and jump up and down and play games all the time. Old people are supposed to sit around talking about the weather and eating and reading the newspaper and complaining about the kids today and telling us to be quiet. Miss Small doesn't do *any* of those things. She's like a big kid. She grew tall, but she never grew up."

"My dad is a doctor," said Emily. "He told me that when old people fall down, they can get hurt really badly. They can even die."

Wow. I didn't know that.

"If Miss Small dies, it will be our fault," Andrea said.

For a while nobody said anything. Maybe Andrea was right, for once in her life.

"We've got to do something," said Emily.

"We should talk to her," Andrea said. "We need to tell her she has to grow up and act mature like other adults."

So all of us—me, Michael, Ryan, Andrea, and Emily—went around the school to the gym. We figured that's where Miss Small would be during recess.

"Shh!" Andrea said as we snuck around the corner. "If Principal Klutz catches us, we could be in big trouble."

Me and Michael and Ryan got down on our hands and knees and pretended to be undercover agents on a secret police mission. It was cool.

Finally we reached the back door to the gym.

"We may have to pick the lock like they always do in police movies," Ryan whispered. "Then they run inside and shout, 'Freeze, dirtbags!'"

"No," Michael said, "in the movies they kick the door in with their feet and shout, 'Freeze, dirtbags!'"

"No, they don't," I told them. "They use bombs to blow the door off the hinges. *Then* they run inside and shout, 'Freeze, dirtbags!'"

"Maybe the door isn't even locked," Emily said.

"The door is *always* locked, dumbhead," I said. "Why else would they have to blow it off the hinges?"

Andrea put her hand on the doorknob and turned it. And you know what? The door opened!

Me and Michael and Ryan ran inside the gym, just like they do in all the police movies.

"Freeze, dirtbags!" we shouted.

And there, in the gym, was the most amazing sight any of us had ever seen.

All the grown-ups who work in the school were there. Every one of them! And they were going *crazy*!

Mr. Klutz, the principal, was doing the Chicken Dance. Our teacher, Miss Daisy, was playing hopscotch. Mrs. Roopy, our librarian, was hula hooping. Ms. Hannah, our art teacher, was jumping rope. Miss Small was clapping her hands and singing that annoying hillbilly music. All the other teachers were doing the limbo and other equally weird stuff.

They all stopped what they were doing

and stared at me and Michael and Ryan.

"What are *you* doing here, boys?" Miss Small asked.

"Uh . . ."

I looked at Ryan and Michael. They were doing that whistling thing you do when you want to pretend you didn't do anything wrong. I didn't know what to do. I didn't know what to say. I had to think fast.

"The question is, what are *you* doing here?" I asked. "Why aren't you all sitting around talking about the weather and eating and drinking coffee and reading the newspaper and doing other grown-up stuff?"

"We're having fun!" Mr. Klutz said.

"Why should you kids have all the fun?" said Miss Daisy.

"Yeah, we want to play too," Mrs. Roopy said.

"This is the only time we have all day to relax," said Ms. Hannah.

"Yeah!" said all the other grown-ups. "Lighten up."

Grown-ups are weird.

Me and Michael and Ryan ran out of there as fast as we could and went back to the playground. I hoped that Miss Daisy wouldn't tell my mom and dad that I called all the grown-ups at our school dirtbags.

Back on the playground, we decided that Miss Small really does have a serious problem. And now it's spreading to all the other teachers. Somehow, we're gonna have to think of a way to make Miss Small grow up and act mature and boring like a normal adult.

But it won't be easy!

Also in the **My Weird School** series

Pb 0-06-050700-4

#1: Miss Daisy Is Crazy!
Something weird is going on! A.J. is a second grader who hates school—and can't believe his teacher hates it too!

Pb 0-06-050702-0

#2: Mr. Klutz Is Nuts!
The second book in this wacky and hilarious series stars A.J. again—and he can't believe his crazy principal wants to climb to the top of the flagpole!

Pb 0-06-050704-7

#3: Mrs. Roopy Is Loopy!
The new librarian at A.J.'s weird school starts dressing up as different historical characters, and A.J. and his friends think she's gone completely off the deep end!

Pb 0-06-050706-3

#4: Ms. Hannah Is Bananas!
A.J.'s art teacher, Ms. Hannah, insists that garbage can be made into art—but even worse, she's making him be partners with know-it-all Andrea!

www.harperchildrens.com
www.dangutman.com

HarperTrophy®
An Imprint of HarperCollinsPublishers